14 Days

NOV. 1 6 1992

MAR   3 1994

JUN   7 1994

JUN 1 5 1994

[JUL] 1 9 1995

NOV 2 4 1995

JUN 2 1 1996

AUG   3 1996

JAN 2 5 2000

JAN 2 5 2002

JUL 3 1 '07

AUG 2 4 07

AUG 1 5 '08

JUL   7 '09

JUN 2 1 2011

WITHDRAWN

W9-BCM-683

THE MYSTERY OF THE MIDNIGHT RAIDER

WRITTEN BY MARY BLOUNT CHRISTIAN
ILLUSTRATED BY JOE BODDY

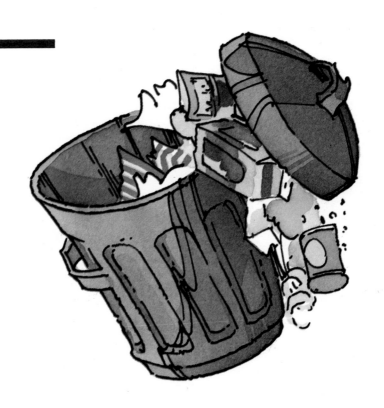

Milliken Publishing Company, St. Louis, Missouri

© 1991 by Milliken Publishing Company

All rights reserved. No part of this book may be used or reproduced in any manner whatsoever without written permission. Printed in the United States of America.

Cover Design by Henning Design, St. Louis, Missouri

Library of Congress Catalog Card Number: 90-064475

ISBN 0-88335-2710 (lib. bdg.) 0-88335-2850 (pbk.)

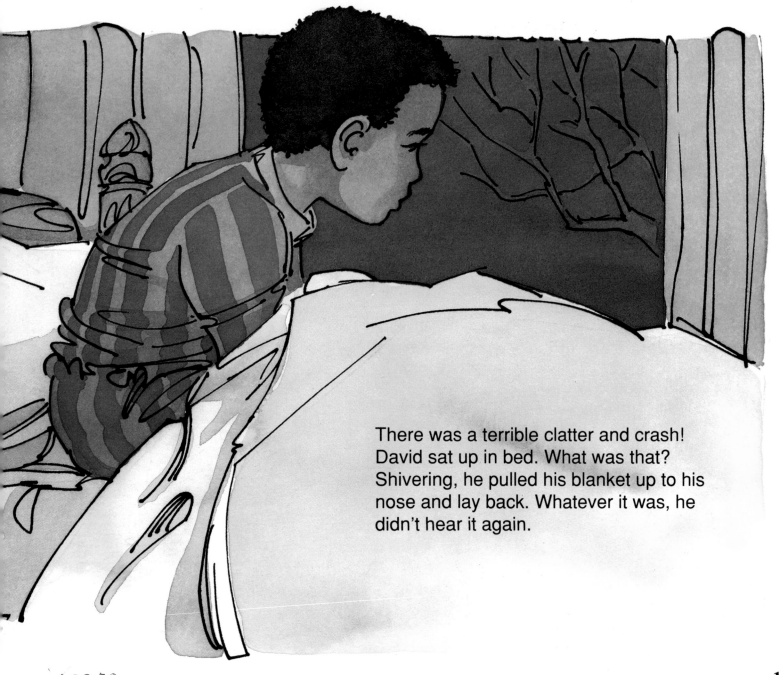

There was a terrible clatter and crash! David sat up in bed. What was that? Shivering, he pulled his blanket up to his nose and lay back. Whatever it was, he didn't hear it again.

j42278

The next morning, he went to the back of the house and found the trash cans overturned. A jumble of orange peels, old Christmas paper, and cans were on the ground. David replaced the trash and closed the lid. He went to see Ann and Walter next door.

"Something turned over our trash cans last night," David said. "The noise woke me up."

"Our trash was spilled, too," Ann said. "We had to clean it up this morning."

"Me too," David said. "And it was so cold that my breath was foggy and my nose nearly froze off."

3

"Oh, David!" Walter said. "It was cold, but not cold enough to freeze your nose!"

They all laughed. "Have you learned to use your new photo and darkroom equipment?" Ann asked. "What a neat Christmas present."

David pulled out some pictures. "My dad helped me develop these. But I think I can do it by myself now."

David showed them pictures he had taken yesterday of the twins and Pedro. They were all making faces and being silly for the camera.

They were laughing at the pictures when Pedro came over. "My, aren't we good looking?" Pedro said when he saw the pictures. He burst out laughing. "I really like that one of you standing on your head, Ann."

"We thought you were coming over earlier," Ann said. "We have the pancake batter ready."

Pedro licked his lips. "I was ready to eat breakfast," he said. "But I had to clean up the back yard. Something knocked over all the trash cans last night."

"Yours too?" Walter said. "I wonder what it was. All the dogs should have been inside on such a cold night."

6

The children ate the pancakes that Mrs. Hatch fixed for them. They thought it was fun to eat together and they were glad there were still a few days left of winter vacation.

"I'm enjoying my race cars and walkie talkies," Pedro said. "But I wish we had a mystery to solve. We need some excitement, don't you think?"

"Why don't you find out what is knocking over the trash cans at night?" Mrs. Hatch said. "That sounds like a good case for the Sherlock Street Detectives."

7

"That doesn't sound like much of a mystery," Ann said. "It's probably just a dog."

"But whose dog?" Mrs. Hatch asked. "Is it a stray dog? Does it need a home? Why is it so hungry that it is out on such a cold night?"

"You're right, Mom!" Walter said. "Let's find out who the dog belongs to. Maybe it's lost. Maybe some little kid is scared because his dog is missing. I would want someone to find Watson for me if he was lost."

Ann laughed. "Oh, Walter. You can always find Watson close to his food bowl. Silly dog," she said.

"Woof!" Watson said.

"See, Ann?" Walter said. "You hurt his feelings."

Ann giggled. "Be serious, Walter. Mom is right. We should find the owner of this dog. We can find out why he is out looking for food on such cold nights. But how?"

"I have an idea," David said. "Why don't we take pictures of the dog when it comes. Then we can show them to the veterinarian. Maybe he will recognize the dog."

"If it is a dog," Ann said. "Maybe it's a raccoon, or an opossum. We live close to some woods, remember."

"There is just one problem," Pedro said. "This always happens in the middle of the night. Who'll stay up and take pictures?"

David said, "Let's go to my house and get my camera. I can set it up so it faces the trash cans. I have a trigger that will make the camera flash when it is pulled.

We can tie one end of a string to the trash can lid and the other end to the trigger. When the lid falls, it will pull the string. Then we will have a picture of the trash can thief."

They all agreed that it was a great idea. After they finished eating, the Detectives set up the camera.

The next morning, all the cans were opened again. Trash was scattered everywhere. Ann and Walter hurried to David's house. Pedro was already there.

"Let's develop the film," David said. "We'll see who the thief is."

David pulled dark curtains over the windows. He turned on a red light and put the film into a series of liquids. He held the film toward the red light. "I see something on the film," he said.

Next, David put the film into a stand. He slid paper onto it. Then he turned on a light for three seconds.

"I still don't see anything," Ann whispered.

"I have to develop it," David said. He put
the paper into a pan of developer fluid.
An image slowly appeared on the paper.

"Oh, look!" Ann said. "It's a brown dog and
her two puppies. They look thin. Poor things."

When the print had dried, the Sherlock Street Detectives dressed warmly. They went to the vet's office and showed him the picture.

He frowned. "That's not a dog," he said. "That is a mother coyote and her pups."

"A coyote!" Ann cried. "In our neighborhood?"

"It was her neighborhood not so long ago," Dr. Wesley said. "We have built our houses where she once lived. Her woods are getting smaller and smaller with each new neighborhood."

"She can't find enough food in the woods. The winter has been cold. Otherwise, she wouldn't come so close to us."

"But I thought coyotes stayed together. What about her mate?" asked Pedro.

"He may have died. Otherwise, he would be with them. Most of her litter probably died, too. Coyotes usually have around eight pups."

"This is terrible!" Ann said. "What can we do to save them? Should we call the zoo?"

"I think it would be best to call the parks and wildlife service," Dr. Wesley said. "They can safely trap the coyote and her pups. They can move them to a place that is not threatened by people. At least not yet."

"But we could feed them," Ann said.

The vet frowned. "That's a bad idea. Make no mistake, Ann, coyotes are not pets. But they are not bad neighbors. Mostly they eat rabbits, rats, and mice. But if they are starving, they will raid trash cans, or even eat a cat or a small dog."

The children gasped, but the vet shook his head. "Coyotes don't understand about pets. Food is food," he said. "They will even scavenge for carrion."

The vet phoned the wildlife service. "They said that it's supposed to snow tonight. If it does, it will be easy to follow the tracks in the morning."

18

19

That evening it began to snow. Ann and Walter left a lamp turned on near the rear window. Its pale light spilled across the trash cans, making it easier to spot the coyote. Ann and Walter took turns watching for the coyote and her pups that night. "Wake up, Ann," Walter whispered. "They're out there."

Ann tiptoed to the window and peeked out. "She's wagging her tail just like a dog," she whispered. "She's so happy to find food."

"Look, Ann," Walter said. "She's letting the pups eat first. She's a good mother." When the pups had finished, the mother coyote ate. When she had finished, she gave out little barks, then one lonely howl.

"How sad, Walter," Ann said. "There was no answer. It really is better to send her where there are other coyotes."

21

There were many tracks around the spilled trash cans. Ms. Turner and Mr. Bader from the wildlife service arrived the next morning. With the Sherlock Street Detectives, they followed the tracks into the woods. The children watched as they set traps near the den. They put food into the traps.

"They will not be hurt," Ms. Turner told the children. "When they get inside to eat the food, the door will shut. We'll take them farther north where they will be safe."

"If more coyotes come into the neighborhoods, we will move them," Mr. Bader said. "If no more come, we will know that they have all left, or that the woods can support them."

"Please, oh please," Ann begged, "let us see them before they are taken away."

"We will pick you up tomorrow morning," Mr. Bader said. "We'll bring you here with us. Then you can say goodbye."

22

j 42278

The next morning Mr. Bader honked his horn and the detectives ran out and climbed into the truck. They rode as far as they could, then walked into the woods.

24

The coyote and her pups were in the trap. She looked at the humans with her cold yellow eyes. She growled when they came nearby and nuzzled her pups behind her.

"She's a good mother," Ann said. "She doesn't understand that we are helping her. She's trying to protect her children."

"By night she will be safe in a new home," Ms. Turner said. "When we open the trap for her, she will run away with her pups. They will quickly adapt to their new home."

That evening, the Sherlock Street Detectives had hot chocolate at Pedro's house. Ann looked out the window and sighed. "It's dark. Mother coyote and her pups are safe in their new home by now. Still, I wonder if there are any more in our woods. I wonder if they'll be all right. I wish there was something we could do to help."

David sipped his chocolate. "I think we can. We can try to preserve part of the woods in their natural state. I think we should get everyone to sign a petition. We have to make people understand how important it is."

Ann put down her cup. "That will be a good project for our science class! I can hardly wait until winter vacation is over and for school to begin."

Walter laughed. "You know what? Neither can I!"

"Woof!" Watson said. He lifted his chin and howled.

The Sherlock Street Detectives laughed and lifted their cups in salute to each other.

Glossary

carrion — dead and decaying flesh

darkroom — a room used for developing film that has been sealed so as not to let in any light

preserve — to keep from harm, to protect

veterinarian — a doctor who specializes in the care and treatment of animals

Vocabulary

Ann	fluid	nearby	service	winter
arrived	foggy	neighborhood	Sherlock	yesterday
barks	freeze	neither	shivering	zoo
batter	frowned	nuzzled	sipped	
blanket	froze	opossum	starving	
bowl	gasped	overturned	support	
breakfast	growled	pancakes	terrible	
breath	Hatch	Pedro	thief	
burst	honked	petition	threatened	
camera	howl	pictures	tiptoed	
carrion	humans	preserve	toward	
chocolate	hungry	project	tracks	
Christmas	hurried	protect	traps	
clatter	hurt	puppies	trigger	
climbed	important	rabbits	twins	
coyote(s)	inside	raccoon	understand	
curtains	jumble	raider	vacation	
darkroom	liquids	recognize	veterinarian	
David	litter	remember	wagging	
detectives	mate	replaced	Walter	
develop	mice	scattered	Watson	
equipment	middle	scavenge	Wesley	
feelings	midnight	school	whispered	
film	mystery	series	wildlife	
flash	natural	serious	window	